PINK AND BLUE

All inquiries should be addressed to:
Barron's Educational Series, Inc.
250 Wireless Boulevard
Hauppauge, NY 11788

International Standard Book Number 0-8120-1921-0

Library of Congress Catalog Card Number 94-14500

PRINTED IN HONG KONG
4567   9927   987654321

GET READY...GET SET...READ!

PINK AND BLUE

by
Foster & Erickson

Illustrations by
Kerri Gifford

BARRON'S

"Oh Sue," said Flute,
"let me give you a clue."

"You would do better
if your food were blue."

"Now Flute," said Sue,
"let's not argue."

"I like pink.
It is so cute!"

"I think you have
too much pink," said Flute.

"And you have
too much blue," said Sue.

"Too much blue! How untrue!
Here's a little blue for you."

"Oh dear," said Sue,
"it is like glue."

"Down the chute,
look out Flute!"

"You can be a brute,"
said Flute.

Blue, blue, pink. . .
and pink, pink, blue. . .

on and on the two argue.

"I think you look good in blue.
I will call you true-blue Sue."

"Well Flute, I think
you look cute in pink."

Now the two like pink *and* blue.

The End

The UTE Word Family

brute
chute
cute
Flute

The UE Word Family

argue
blue
clue
glue
Sue
true-blue
untrue

Sight Words

out
two
call
dear
food
good
give
pink
think
would
better
little

Dear Parents and Educators:

Welcome to *Get Ready...Get Set...Read!*

We've created these books to introduce children to the magic of reading.

Each story in the series is built around one or two word families. For example, *A Mop for Pop* uses the OP word family. Letters and letter blends are added to OP to form words such as TOP, LOP, and STOP. As you can see, once children are able to read OP, it is a simple task for them to read the entire word family. In addition to word families, we have used a limited number of "sight words." These are words found to occur with high frequency in the books your child will soon be reading. Being able to identify sight words greatly increases reading skill.

You might find the steps outlined on the facing page useful in guiding your work with your beginning reader.

We had great fun creating these books, and great pleasure sharing them with our children. We hope *Get Ready...Get Set...Read!* helps make this first step in reading fun for you and your new reader.

Kelli C. Foster, PhD
Educational Psychologist

Gina Clegg Erickson, MA
Reading Specialist

Guidelines for Using *Get Ready...Get Set...Read!*

Step 1.   Read the story to your child.

Step 2.   Have your child read the Word Family list aloud several times.

Step 3.   Invent new words for the list. Print each new combination for your child to read. Remember, nonsense words can be used (*dat, kat, gat*).

Step 4.   Read the story *with* your child. He or she reads all of the Word Family words; you read the rest.

Step 5.   Have your child read the Sight Word list aloud several times.

Step 6.   Read the story *with* your child again. This time he or she reads the words from both lists; you read the rest.

Step 7.   Your child reads the entire book to you!

Titles in the
Get Ready...Get Set...Read! Series